AMAZON
DIARY

Alex Winters

Chicago

Caracas

VEZUELA

Puerto Ayacucho

Parima

YANOMAMI LAND

Guyana

Brazil

me pilot

Chicago

Parima →
(the camp)

Jungle
↓

Captain's Log
STARDATE: Dec.18
(Kirk would approve)

I can't believe its finally today. I, Alex Winters, am actually sitting in a Cessna 185, <u>next</u> to the pilot, flying over the **Amazon Jungle!!!** This **is** really happening, right? I mean, who else in the whole sixth grade is even leaving Chicago for Christmas? Much less flying down to South America to visit parents who are searching for a "lost" tribe of Indians? I'm glad Mom & Dad see that I want to be an <u>anthropologist</u> too, but I'll have to convince Mom that I'm old enough to go with them into the jungle, looking for the tribe **Yanomamis**—the so-called "Fierce People"—I wonder if they'll shrink my head. I wonder if there are any left. I wonder if I'll even get to see one before I go home. That would be cool.

Whoa! Its getting dark outside fast! bump

Mike the pilot said we're gonna have to fly around a big thunderstorm to get to Mom & Dad's camp. I'm glad they have airsick bags on board. When Grandpa gave me this book he said to write down everything that happens as it happens. Right now its getting really bumpy. The plane is shaking. Mike said to put down the book and tighten my seatbelt

Dear Diary, Dear God, Dear Whoever may find this—
   I'm alone in the forest now. As far as I know, I was in a plane crash, but I'm O.K. I've been in the dark for a few hours and my head really hurts. The last thing I remember Mike saying is that we have to try landing. We're by a river now, and the right wing is sheared off. Mike is out cold but at least he's breathing. There's blood on his head and his leg looks pretty twisted. If I move him I'll need to make a splint first. We did it in Boy Scouts, last year. I just hope I remember how. I don't know what to do— except pray a lot. I smell gas fumes.

12:30 A.M.
   I found my watch—it was in my backpack. I got some bandages and stuff out of it to make a splint for Mike's leg. I'm gonna try to move him in a minute. Please, God, are you there? Are you listening? What am I doing? What am I supposed to do? Are Mom and Dad coming?   Am I gonna die here?

3:15 A.M.
   Sitting next to a fire I made with a sterno can from the plane's emergency pack. Most of the wood is wet. I'm so exhausted from pulling Mike out of the plane I could collapse but every peep and squawk from the jungle shakes me up again. I probably shouldn't sleep anyway. They'll fly over soon and I'll need to wave something at them. They're on their way, I know they are. Mom says the rainforest is getting smaller and smaller. And they have all kinds of tracking systems now.
   Please, God, help is on the way, right?   Please

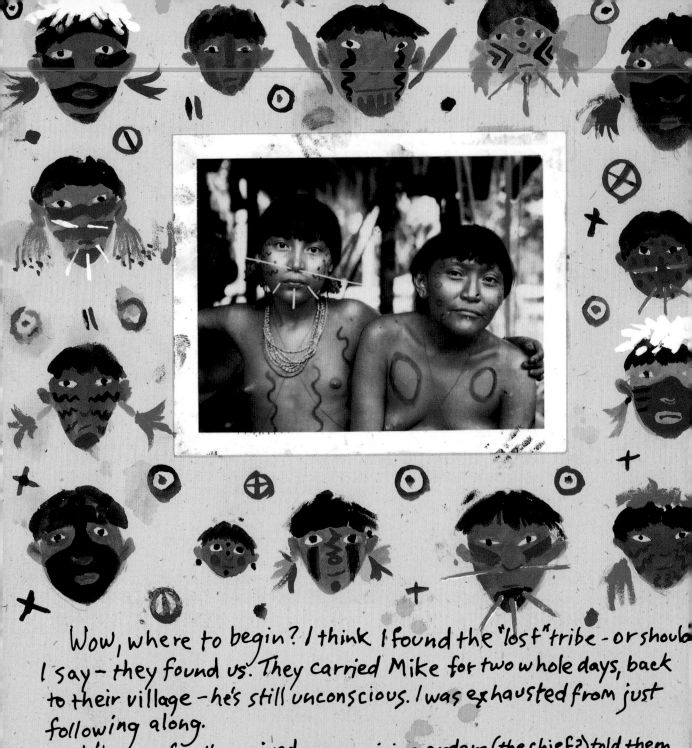

Wow, where to begin? I think I found the "lost" tribe - or should I say - they found us. They carried Mike for two whole days, back to their village - he's still unconscious. I was exhausted from just following along.

When we finally arrived a man giving orders (the chief?) told them where to lay Mike down. Then he came over with his arms out and hugged me. He motioned to a hammock where I could rest.

I'm still alive after 3 days with them so I guess I'm safe. But I wonder if they've ever seen anyone with pale skin or blonde hair? or wearing clothes? What do they see when they look at me?

Dec. 22   11:30 A.M.
    There's not much I can do
about getting out of here until
Mike wakes up. I'm glad I've
got the Walkman recorder,
Polaroid camera, and all my
paint stuff so I can record
all this. No one would
believe me otherwise.

↑   I'll start with view from my hammock. This is the
family "next door." The chief wasn't around when I took
this, but that's one of his daughters. She seems sick.
I heard her moaning last night. She is kinda yellow
and always shivering. I hope it's not malaria.

9:35 P.M.
    I got her to take some of
my malaria pills when she
saw me take mine, but
her older brother
pulled her away.
What's his problem?

Gosh, it's hot here

River

The Shapono

boats are small, made of bark strips or dug out logs

Families sleep in hammocks around a fire

The moms keep the fire going

tobacco drying

"Shapono" was the first word I learned. Our rescuers kept saying it louder and louder like I would get it if they said it loud enough. I finally did when they brought us here and pointed to it. It's like a giant, baseball field-size donut. It's home for now

Garden

Path

entrance

an old man lives here

closed by a wall to outside

roof slants down

River

more garden

Taponowateri is what they call themselves and also their village, like if I called my turf Alexland.

they killed a gator here

en to center

inside

Outside

OPEN AREA

path to river

entrance

big fires here

Kids play in here

tobacco

Garden

banana grove

they hang all their stuff on the wall

its smokey under the roof from all the fires

Jungle

QUIET -please

Dec. 24 5:30 A.M.

I'm awake because I still haven't got the hang of sleeping here (I don't mean the hammock) Its more like "napping" during a break in the racket. Shouting, arguing, yelling, cackling, chanting, story-telling. LONG storytelling - babies crying, and kids playing all night long! Don't they have school nights in the jungle? And it gets cold too. I don't think they've discovered blankets yet so the women keep the fires going all night long. The men yell at them when they die down.

The men usually go hunting at first light and don't come back until they have something - mostly monkeys and parrots. Yesterday I saw them chase an alligator for over an hour until they could finally spear it on the riverbank. It seems like they hunt anything that moves.

Now that its light I can find my way to the "bathroom," otherwise known as the woods. (If this was Chicago I'd probably go out and spell my name in the snow.)

I try to help out around
here whenever I can.
← This guy fixing the roof
really liked it when I started
passing the palm leaves to
him. He almost fell off, though,
when I turned up my Walkman
to "share" the Grateful Dead.
I thought everybody liked
them...

It was fun showing the kids
a magazine I was bringing
to Mom. They turned it around
and around until they came
to a picture of the Royal Family.
It reminded me of that
Movie, "Trading Places."

I could just picture my friends
hanging out in Buckingham Palace.
And the queen taking a bath in the river.
Watch out for piranha, Your Majesty...

Ra Ra Ra
Ra Ra
Ra
Grrrr

I gave her sister the malaria pills

Everyone always knows where I am because the dogs bark whenever they see me.

The river is my favorite place - it's always busy. Thes ladies are cooling off with a quick dip on their way home from the banana grove. The women and girls do so much work, but always seem to be having fun.

Piranha!
Vicious but delicious!
I wonder if they would say that about me?...

The boys "play-hunt" for lizards along the beach
and are always looking for turtle eggs. They find them
by poking an arrow into the sand until it comes up
with yolk on it.

...al
piranha
teeth

PTUUI

arrow point for fishing

Humans!
taste just like
chicken...

Things I Don't Like About The JUNGLE

① Trees with an attitude

② Electric caterpillars →

③ Fire ants

especially the ones living in firewood

Like eels, but they climb trees

④ Poison frogs

wanna pet me? heh, heh —

Touch 'em and you'll croak!

⑤ No-see-'ems - but you sure feel 'em

⑥ Head Lice   even in the best o

Yeah, I already have 'em

⑦ Snakes - the little black ones kill ya quick, but the big, fat ones squeeze you till you can't breathe (sounds like Aunt Edna)

Dec. 25

Speaking of snakes, I thought I felt one in my hammock this morning. I remembered that line from the movies, "SNAKE! Don't move a muscle!" So I held perfectly still. When I cracked open an eye I saw the girl I've been giving my malaria pills to. She was touching the hair on my arm. I was glad to see she was alive and well and not a killer snake. Not knowing what else to do, I said, "Hi." "Hi," she said back. I touched my arm hair and said, "hair." "Hair," she repeated perfectly. Slowly her mouth, sticks and all, widened into a smile.

I wasn't sure what to do next, but then she opened her pouch and pulled out what I guess was her idea of breakfast in bed. It was a really _moving_ gesture. Really moving. Now what?

I smiled and sat up, then patted my chest and said, "Alex."

She glanced around, then slowly whispered, "Wakima."

My grandmother used to say "food is a form of love." Somehow, after Wakima roasted those grubs I could've sworn they tasted just like chicken.

The pills seem to be working on her - good thing we have a lot of 'em.

* Good news - Mike just woke up long enough to drink some water.

Merry Christmas, Alex

Dec. 27

    I thought "cool" was flying down to South America all by myself. **Hah.** COOL is sitting in a dug-out canoe, floating down a jungle river with the chief of a "lost" tribe hunting for alligators. Wakima's father invited me along by putting a paddle in my hands. I'm on the "paddling team" with his son (I call him "Bub" because he won't tell me his name). "Bub" still acts kinda weird to me — I think he's jealous of me getting so much attention from his dad and his sister. But, hey, it's too cool being here to let that bother me.

Anyway, it was a great day on the river, and we caught two big gators. We were heading back when the chief pointed to something in the water ahead of us. It was a **tapir,** a giant pig-size animal with a long snout. It surfaced next to our boat, then dove underneath it, and came up on the other side — swimming and splashing through the water for dear life. We zigzagged across the river in hot pursuit, finally closing in on it. Then a spear and two arrows shot out. My eyes could follow its flight through the air and into the tapir's neck. I never saw anything so big die before.

Dec. 28

There's a buzz in the village today. The tapir is being cut up and smoked and the gators are all roasting. The women have been bringing in lots of this fruit they call **rasha**. It's mealy like a chestnut but sweeter. Great with gator.

I think there's a big party in the works. Maybe it's Yanomami Thanksgiving. I mean, what else do you do with a smoked tapir, 10 gators, and a zillion boiled rashas except have a **rasha festival!!!**

gator head →

↑ rashas

It's funny but the adults here don't seem anything like adults. They're dressing for the party by painting themselves with mashed-up berries. They would love Halloween.

Ra-sha Ra-sha Ra-sha

This guy borrowed
my signal mirror. I doubt
if he's ever seen himself
before, except in the river.

Yup, tastes just
like chicken

Oh my gosh—
Now a bunch of guys are waving their arms and shouting toward the sky. It must be their religious practice.

Dad told me that when they want to contact the spirit world they grind a certain plant into a powder, then blow the powder into each other's nose. Then they stumble around like their heads are killing them, green snot pours out of their noses, and they usually throw up. Then they call out to the universe.

I hear shouts and hollers coming from the forest. I think company's coming. It's all making me a little nervous but Wakima is having fun. She's trying to get me to follow her out of the shapono. She must know what's happening. The shouts are getting closer. What's up?

A little later —

At first I didn't see all the people. But there they were. The guests had arrived. Their decorations blended in with the colors of the forest. They wore feathers and skins of animals that I have never seen before.

When I tried to take pictures I had to wait because my hands were shaking so much. I wasn't scared or anything - its just that it was all so beautiful. So amazing. Tears even came to my eyes.

Wow. Where am I?

and the Oscar for best-dressed goes to...

Noon

The visitors' kids soon found me, and got that "What-planet-are-you-from?" look in their eyes. They surrounded me and seemed curious about this book. I drew this monkey to break the ice. They smiled and said "pasho." Then I drew this bird. "Pioma, pioma, pioma," they all whispered. They probably had never seen paper or pencils before. I handed the book to them and this is what they did

Pasho

Monkey

Pioma bird

and that

they drew this in my sketchbook

They drew this exotic creature in a hammock.....me.

my book →

↳He was the best

I drew this big snake which
kinda scared them. They all
whispered "Rahara, Rahara." Then I
remembered the story Mom told me - they
believe there's a monster serpent in the jungle
called "Rahara." Mom says it probably comes from their fear
of the giant anaconda, a snake that grows up to 40 ft. long and
really does live in the rivers here. I'd sure love to see one...
.....in the zoo

Now every**body**'s singing and dancing and hooting and hollering. They're all swinging their clubs and axes in the air and laughing, laughing, laughing. I feel like I'm on Mars.

it's getting

around here

feathers that flew off dancers

KIDS follow their moms

YEE-HAAA

bow & arrows

Items on the

Yanomami Stock Exchange

arrow points

beads

leopard hat
jaguar

baskets

ear doo-dads

axe heads

feathers

Monkey fur ar

The dancing finally ended and everyone rested for a while
Now the men have gathered for what appears to be a big trading sessio
All the trade stuff is piled in the center of a big circle, with the visitors o
one side and the "home team" on the other. Wakima's dad is trying to
trade a bow & arrow set for a visitor's fur hat, but the visitor wants more ar
thrown in for the deal. Everyone on the sidelines is giving their opinion
it seems ("you're getting rooked!" or maybe – "Hold on to that jaguar! It's g
ting harder to come by!") It's their spectator sport, I guess. This cou
go on for hours. I better go check on Mike.

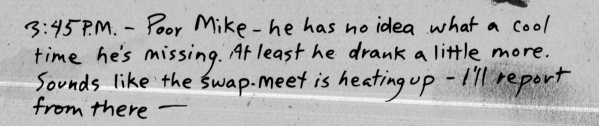

3:45 P.M. – Poor Mike – he has no idea what a cool time he's missing. At least he drank a little more. Sounds like the swap-meet is heating up – I'll report from there —

4:30 P.M. – Whoa!
   Things suddenly changed and all the traders are angry now! A woman came into the swap meet and started yelling at her husband – probably that he was an idiot for getting cheated. Now everybody's up on their feet and grabbing their clubs. And they're all yelling at each other. Uh-oh....
      Looks like the party's over.

I almost got whacked when I took this pic. They all turned and yelled at me when the flash went off.

The air is electric here now. Things sure have turned ugly fast.
Something exploded between Bub (Wakima's brother) and a big guy
from the visiting village and now its a free-for-all. The big guy keeps
snarling at Bub and grabbing Katoma, Bub's other sister, like he's
trying to take her. Then Bub grabs her back and hits the guy. I wish I
could help Katoma-she's so upset. Bub just whacked "Snarly" with his club.
What guts-he couldn't be more than 14 and Snarly's a grown-up. The
visiting women have grabbed their babies and are hiding behind their men,
who are standing together with their bows drawn. Bub and his dad, the
chief, are leading our guys now. They've gotten Katoma away from Snarly
and are forcing him and the other visitors out of the shapono.

Poor Katoma —
They're pulling at
her from both directions

They're leaving now, thank God. A few guys have bloody
heads from the clubbing, and Katoma is a mess, but at least
it's over. Or is it? I haven't seen Wakima during all this. She
may be hiding. I wouldn't blame her. I want to make sure
that she's o.k. though.

6:30 P.M.
Something terrible has happened. After looking everywhere
for Wakima, I gestured to her dad, "Where's Wakima?" He
looked alarmed. The whole village started searching and pretty soon they
were all in a panic. I think the visitors took her.

Dec. 29 11:00 A.M.

It's hard to write now, but I have to do something. I'm very scared. The babies are crying - even the parrots are crying. The men are no longer dads, husbands, hunters or gardeners - they're warriors. They've lined up in the center of the shapono and are taking turns charging at a straw dummy. They let out blood curdling screams as they hack at their "enemy" with clubs and axes. It's like a psyche-up for a big game - but this is no game. I'm recording it all on my Walkman. There's no way I can take pictures now.   I wish I were invisible.

Bub is acting kinda weird. He and his two buddies are in a corner sharpening arrow points. He's too young to be a warrior, but he really got shamed yesterday when they kidnaped his sister from right under his nose.

If there is going to be a war, I just hope that no one dies, and that they bring back Wakima.

Uh-oh — Bub & his pals just sneaked out under the back wall with their weapons — I'll finish this later——

Bub and his friends were going after Wakima on their own. [t]ailed them silently for about an hour until I stumped my toe. [the]y turned and drew their bows but then saw that it was me. [B]ub looked annoyed but he motioned for me to keep up with them [an]d to be very quiet. Just after dark we reached the edge of the camp that the visitors - now the "enemy" - had made for the night. It was easy to spot Wakima with a full moon out.

In the camp Snarly and another guy were fighting over Wakima.
Bub seemed clueless about what to do next, and pretty soon his pals
were making signs of backing out. Then I got an idea. It was the
old "fake right, run left," but with a Walkman twist.
I think I invented a new sign language
trying to explain my strategy to
Bub & friends. Taking a big gulp
and praying they understood,
I went into action...

going around

through the jungle.

lean-to and hammocks in the t...

dashed in for...

...then...

Wakima

I took off alone

① I took off alone

fires

lean-to le...

Me

"pals"

⑤ Bub waited here till all the men left the camp

⑥ We quickly found each other and

to the far side of the enemy camp.

② I put my tape recorder in a tree, and aimed the speaker toward the camp

③ I rewound the tape to the spot where I hoped was the recording of the war cries from this morning's rally in our village. I pushed the button...

the enemy warriors grabbed their weapons and ran toward the noise

then.....

ran for my life!

camp fires

lean-to

lean-to

in the trees

and hammocks

④ ran for my life!

The sound of our warriors' screams and howls suddenly blasted through the jungle night. It even shocked me.

then ran like the wind for the next hour

It was hard for me to keep up with the others. I had fallen pretty far behind when I sensed someone chasing us. Then a spear flew past my ears! I could see Wakima and Bub ahead, walking on a log to cross a deep ravine. If I could get there quick, we could shove the log off the edge. I leaped for it, but a hand grabbed my shirt tail. Snarly —

I yelled for help, but there was no one in sight. They were long gone.

Then Bub stepped out of the shadows, with an arrow aimed right at us. Snarly had no other weapons now, and was trying to use me for a shield. But I wouldn't let him. Bub was looking for a clear shot when Wakima appeared. She yelled something across to Snarly and he yelled back. Bub answered him, lowering his bow. Suddenly,

Snarly pushed me forward and fled into the night. I scrambled across the log, knocked it off the edge, and hugged my friends. Then we ran like mad.

We finally stopped to rest alongside a stream, and I had a chance to take off my sneakers. Somehow, a tiny frog had crawled into one, shimmied down to my toes and died. He must have been there a long time. I guess I've been distracted.

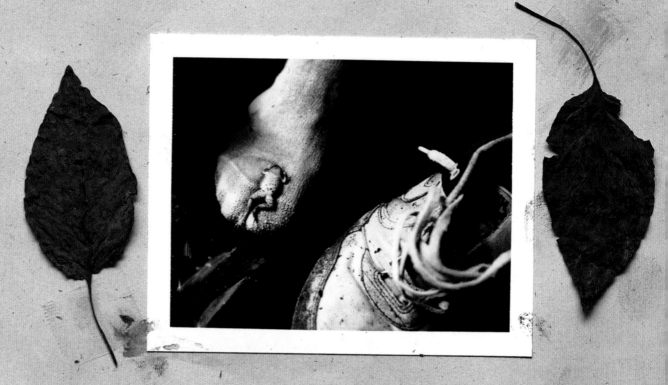

He was our only casualty

Just before dawn we ran into the war party coming from our village, led by Wakima's & Bub's father. You should've seen the looks on the warriors' faces — surprise, disbelief, joy, amazement. Actually, I think it can be summed up in one word — R·E·L·I·E·F.

Dec. 30

Boy, did it feel good to walk into our shapono, sort of like soldiers coming home from the war. Wakima's family and friends were all over us – in fact, the whole village came out. Then a strange sound hit my ears – English. "Alex, you're alive!" It was Mike, the pilot, awake at last. He laughed at seeing me all painted up. I told him some of what he had missed while he was "out-of-it." He was shocked to hear that we had already been there for almost two weeks. He said we had to leave at first light tomorrow and find our way back to the plane crash site, because the emergency radio transmitter would've sent out distress signals from there, and that's where any rescuers would go. It had been a long time since I'd thought about being "rescued," or even leaving. I'm using the rest of the day today to work on my diary and catch up on all of yesterday's events. And then to say my goodbyes.

I'm not really ready to leave, but I know that what I'm taking with me is what matters. I love the people here, and the way they live – like one giant family. I love the forest, and the river, and the night. I love my friends – Bub, his dad, Wakima. I love feeling accepted. I don't think I need anything else except knowing this.

I'm finishing this diary now in Seat 2A on the way back to Chicago. The story of our "rescue" was such big international news that the airline put us in 1st class, like we're celebrities. I can't say I'm unhappy about going home, but I feel a part of me is still back in Taponowateri. I'm glad Mom & Dad aren't worried about me anymore. They had been scouring the area around the crash site for a couple of days when we showed up with our Yanomami friends. Now that was a moment they won't forget soon.

Dad had learned a bit of their language and talked as long as he could to the chief until we had to leave in the helicopters. He said the chief called me "son" and was proud of me. And Bub called me a "clever" warrior and a fine brother. Then Ukima quietly came forward. Wiping away tears, she fastened her beads around my neck and hugged me. Dad told her that when I finish school in Chicago-ateri I could come back and visit her in the land of the Yanomami. And I will.

To learn more about the Yanomamis, and their current situation, please write to:
Amazonia Foundation
P.O. Box 122
Summit, N.J. 07901
U.S.A.